Black History Adventures
Greenwood and Tulsa'

Dedicated to Bro. Walter A. Robinson

An Educator, Change Agent, Leader, and Father.
September 26, 1952 - June 9th, 2019

This Adventure is brought to you by the creators of Black Wall Street the Board Game. Remember. Relearn. Rebuild.

Published by
iMi Press

It's the first day of Summer Vacation in West Harlem. Rose and Rodney have worked hard in school all year and now it's time to have fun!

"Rose! Rose! Rose!" Rodney yells to his big sister with joy. "Ask Mom if we can go to the movies today. I want to see the new Black Panther."

"Why do I have to ask?" Rose sighs. " You're the one that loves the movies."

"Oh come on! You know you're her favorite." Rodney pleads.

Rose and Rodney's parents come to the doorway holding a mysterious treasure chest.

"Hey Mom, Rodney wants to go to the movies," Rose says. Rodney jumps up and crosses his arms. "Hey! Thanks for nothing." He looks towards the door. "Well, mom can we?!"

"Sorry love, no movies today. Your Dad and I need to go into the store but we have a special surprise for you," Mom says.

Dad waddles in with a heavy trunk in his hands and sweat on his forehead. "This Treasure Chest belonged to your Great Grandfather and has been in our family for over 100 years. Maybe more!"

Rodney lays back down in bed and covers his face with a pillow. "An old treasure chest? I hope there's a magical Playstation inside."

Rose jumps up with excitement "Rodney, it's history! It's our family legacy! Thanks Dad."

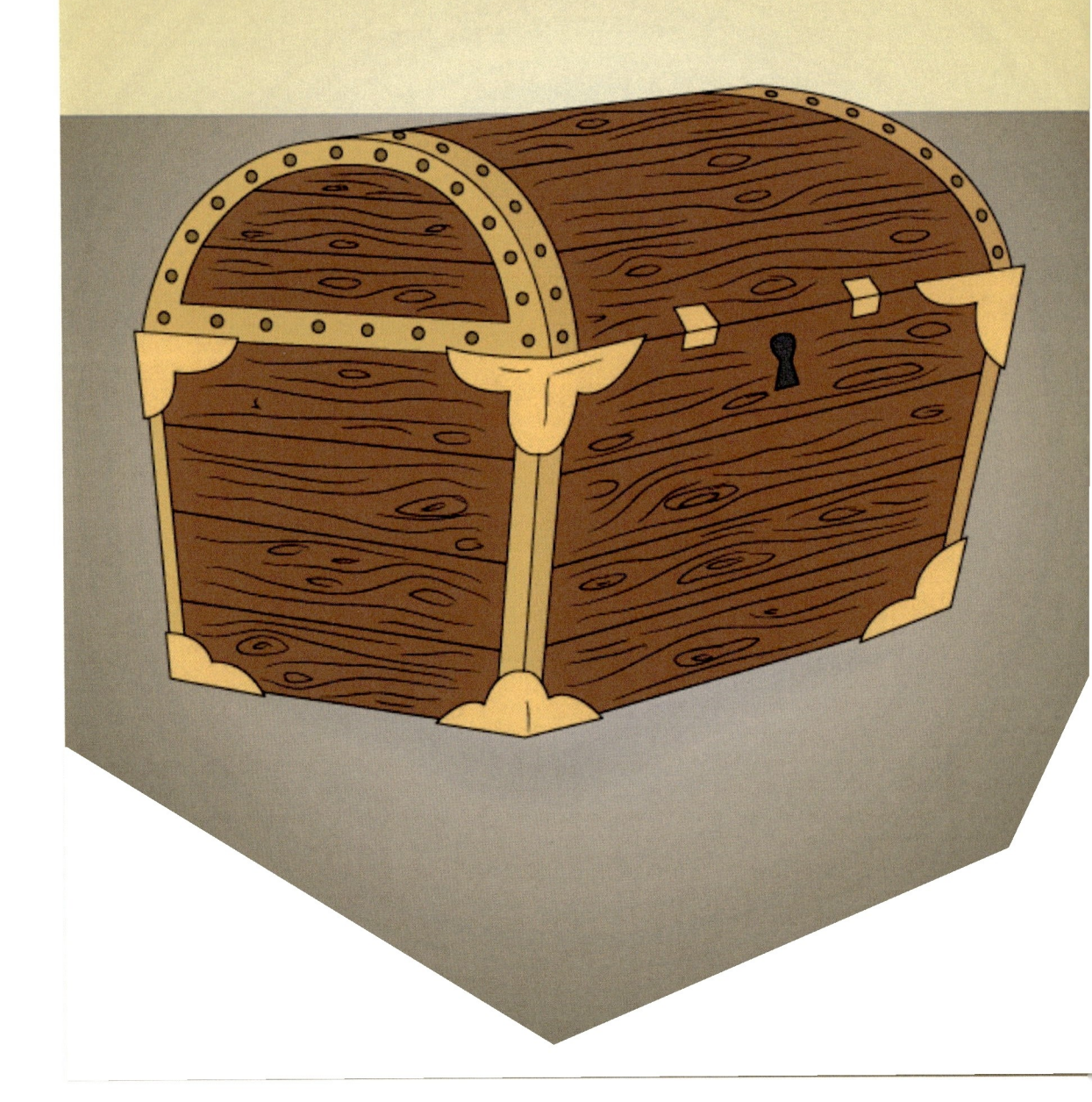

"Why do you have to go to work today? Rodney asks. "Let someone else do it."

Mom gives Rodney a big hug. "It's our business, Rodney. The Family Business and someday it will belong to you and your sister."

"We have to go, we love you. Rodney, no movies and no dancing," Dad says sternly.

Rose and Rodney both respond. " Yes sir."

Rose and Rodney take a look at their Great Grandfather's treasure chest.

"There's a message," Rose discovers.

Rodney wiggles closer, curious. "Well what's it say?

Rose reads the message. " This trunk is the sole property of Walter A Robinson or the descendants of. To activate this trunk a person of royal blood must recite the honorable creed."

Rose sits back. " I don't know Rodney this a bit much."
"I'm not doing puzzles and worksheets all day Rose. They gave us this thing so let's use it!" Rodney cheered.
Rose and Rodney read the creed aloud together.

The Creed
I am the master of my mind.
I am the keeper of my health.
I am the master of time.
I am the maker of wealth.

The treasure chest begins to rumble and pulls Rose and Rodney in. "Rodney what did you do?!" Rose screams.

Rose and Rodney fly through the sky in a magical whirlwind and land on streets paved with gold. Rodney touches the ground and looks around. "Woahhh is this gold? Rose is this where the Wiz lives?" Rose fixes her hair. "You watch too many movies Rodney. We must be in..."

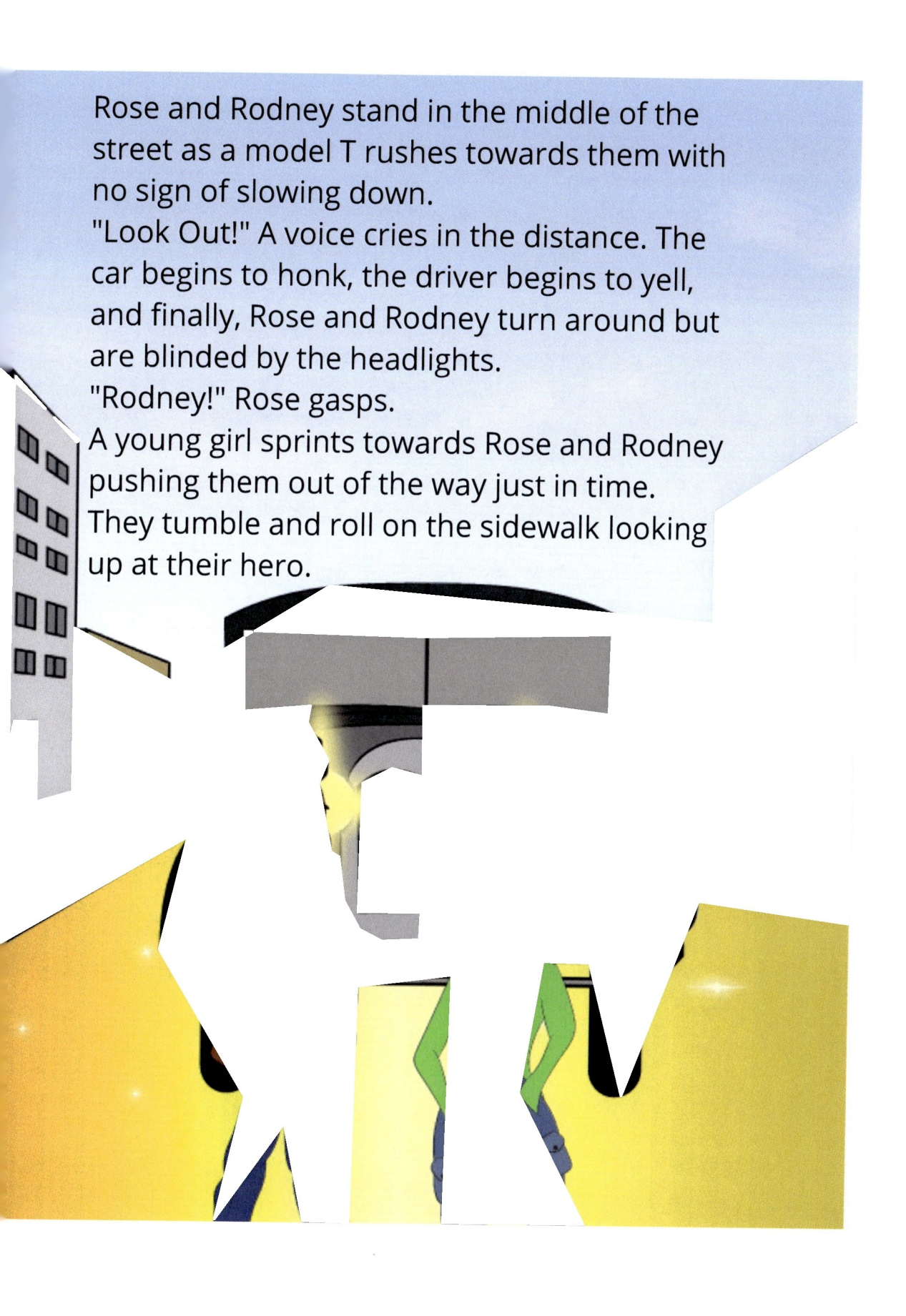

Rose and Rodney stand in the middle of the street as a model T rushes towards them with no sign of slowing down.

"Look Out!" A voice cries in the distance. The car begins to honk, the driver begins to yell, and finally, Rose and Rodney turn around but are blinded by the headlights.

"Rodney!" Rose gasps.

A young girl sprints towards Rose and Rodney pushing them out of the way just in time. They tumble and roll on the sidewalk looking up at their hero.

Elliot & Hooker Clothing C

What in the world were you two doing in the street? You almost got ran over by Mr. Berry," Mabel yells.

"He's a busy man. The town pilot and owns most of the buses around here. If you got places to go Berry's the man to know," she says proudly.

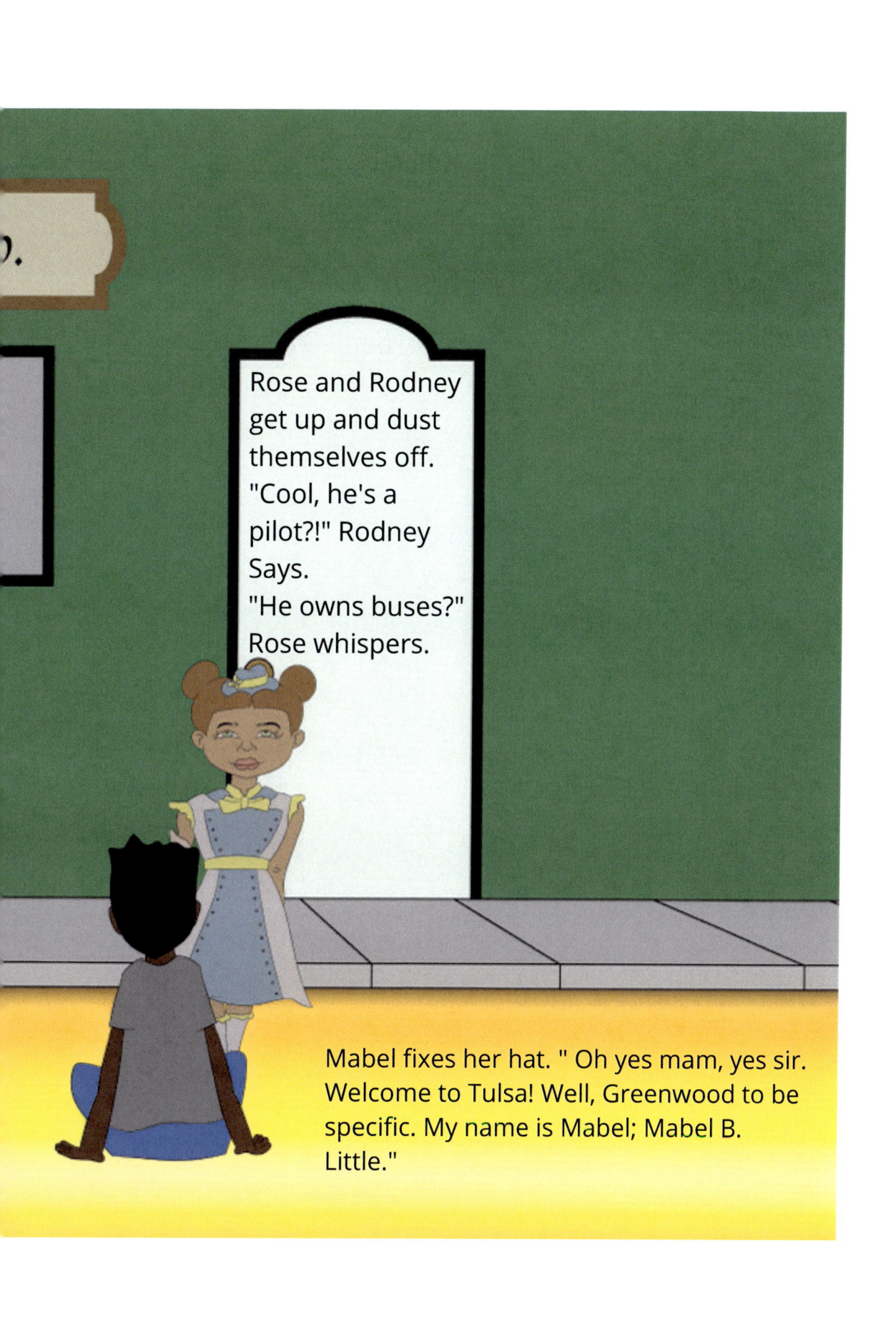

Rose and Rodney get up and dust themselves off.
"Cool, he's a pilot?!" Rodney Says.
"He owns buses?" Rose whispers.

Mabel fixes her hat. " Oh yes mam, yes sir. Welcome to Tulsa! Well, Greenwood to be specific. My name is Mabel; Mabel B. Little."

"Thanks for saving us! I'm Rose and this is my little brother Rodney," Rose explains.
Mabel smiles with excitement. "Pleasure to meet you, Rose and Rodney. Now first things first, we need to get you two into some new clothes."
Rodey empties his pockets. "But we don't have any money."
"Trust me I've been there before. Don't you worry Lil Rodney, I don't know about where you're from but we take care of our own in Greenwood!" Mabel Cheered.

Elliot & Hooker Clothing Co.

Mabel takes them inside to get some new clothes suited for 1914.
"With these new clothes, you'll look sharper than a steak knife!" Mabel gushed.
Rodney examines the clothes. "These look like old clothes to me."
The group leaves the store and runs into a woman carrying boxes of flat irons and hair products.
"Madam CJ!" Mabel Yells.
"Hey, Mabel! You on your way to the shop today? I could use some extra hands with Juneteenth next week."
"Yes, mam! Just showing these young folks around town," Mabel Says.
Madam CJ Walker takes a look at Rose and Rodney. "Bring your friends, They can use a hair cut."

Rose, Rodney, and Mabel all follow Madam CJ Walker to her up-scale beauty salon.

Madam CJ Walker opens up the door and yells "Look who I found giving a tour around Greenwood!"

"Hey, Mabel!" The Ladies in the salon yell.

Rodney looks around. " Hey it's all-girls here, what about my hair?"

Mabel laughs, "I'll take you across the street to the New State Barber Shop. Rose, take a seat and live like a Queen."

After their hair cut Rose and Rodney change into their new clothes from 1914. They look good!

Mabel claps and cheers. " Now y'all look like you're from Greenwood!"

Rodney smiles and gives a smooth spin. "Let's go see a movie!"

"Rodney..." Rose glares.

"Great idea Rodney, I know just the place," Mabel said.

They all turn to the Boss."Thanks Madam CJ!"

Rodney smiles at Rose and they run across the street to Williams' Dreamland theatre.

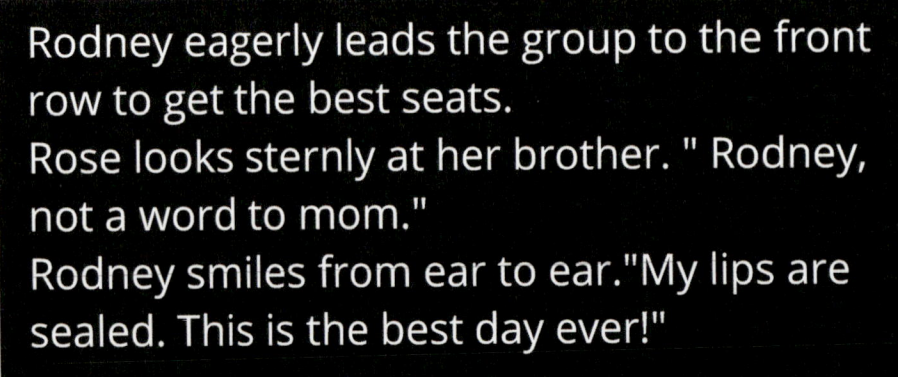

Rodney eagerly leads the group to the front row to get the best seats.
Rose looks sternly at her brother. " Rodney, not a word to mom."
Rodney smiles from ear to ear."My lips are sealed. This is the best day ever!"

"Awww man that's it. The movie was only 20 minutes," Rodney Sighs.

"This is one of the long ones! Most movies are 10-15 minutes. Where are you from again?"

Rose and Rodney look at each other. "Uhhhhh"

Mabel shrugs it off. "Anyway, y'all want to eat the best BBQ in Tulsa?"

Rose sighs in relief. "Yes, but Mabel we don't have any money."

Rodney jumps up." I have an idea!"

Rodney leads the group quickly out of the theatre.
Rose gasping behind him. "What's the plan Rodney?"
Rodney looks back and motions his sister to follow. "Just trust me, I got this."
Rodney leads them to a band playing on the street. There's a drummer, a saxophone player, and someone on the harmonica.
Rodney looks back at his sister and smiles. "Remember, not a word to Mom."
Before his sister can say otherwise Rodney joins in with the taps in his feet and the groove in his shoulders. The music gets louder and a small crowd begins to build up clapping to the beat.
Rose sighs, "When in Greenwood."

Rose Sings
"When You're in Greenwood
The streets are paved with Gold
When You're in Greenwood
The Hearts are Never Cold
When You're in Greenwood
With Rodney and Rose
When You're in Greenwood
A story Never Told"

The band passes around an empty hat to the cheering crowd who drop coins and bills inside as they sing along with Rose. When the hat comes back around it's full!
"Thanks for the jam session young man. Here's your cut for your gifts. Come back tomorrow!" says the Saxophone player.
Rose takes the money. "Don't talk to strangers Rodney. Thank you sir."
"Let's Eat!" Rodney Cheers.

Rose, Rodney, and Mabel skip proudly down the street to the best BBQ in Tulsa, Uncle Steve's BBQ.

Mabel opens up the menu. " There it is, the McGabe Family Special! Edwin McGabe was a politician who really put Oklahoma on the map for folks like us. He said Oklahoma could have everything we ever wanted and more. So here is the McGabe Family Special!"

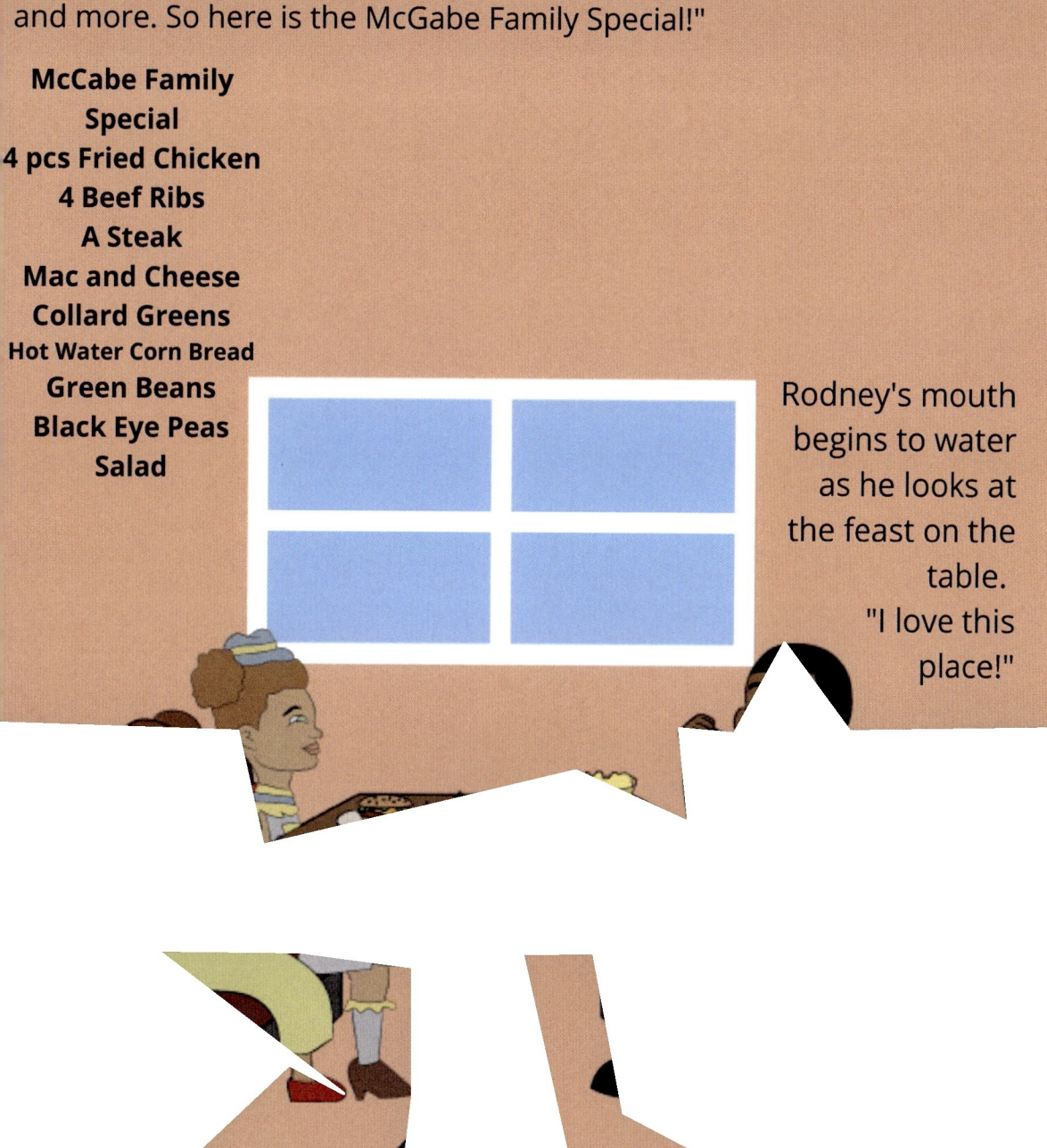

McCabe Family Special
4 pcs Fried Chicken
4 Beef Ribs
A Steak
Mac and Cheese
Collard Greens
Hot Water Corn Bread
Green Beans
Black Eye Peas
Salad

Rodney's mouth begins to water as he looks at the feast on the table.
"I love this place!"

15 minutes later the only thing left is bones and bbq sauce on Rodney's cheeks as Uncle Steve himself comes to the table.
"How was your meal young ones? Any room for dessert?"
Rose politely wipes her mouth." Everything was delicious sir, thank you, but I couldn't eat one more bite." She slumps down in her seat and holds her tummy.
"For once I agree with my sister," groans Rodney as he slumps down in his seat with a smile.
They pay the check and waddle out of Uncle Steve's BBQ,happy.

Mabel takes a look at the sky. " I have to get home before the sun goes down. Y'all have a place to stay?"
Rose and Rodney look at each other and shake their heads.
" Y'all can stay at Gurley's Hotel, he'll take good care of you," Mabel says with a smile.

They walk into Gurley's fancy hotel with clean wood floors, custom furniture, and diamonds hanging from the ceiling.
"Wow does he really own this whole building?" Rodney whispers.
O.W Gurley himself walks up and greets them, "It's not about what you own young man , it's about who you serve. Hey Little Mabel they told me you had some friends in town."
"Yes sir. I need to get home before the sun goes down. Do you have any rooms available?" Mabel asks.

O.W Gurley motions them towards the stairs. "You know I'll take care of them, that's a Greenwood promise."

Rose and Rodney settle into a room of their own at the Gurley Hotel. With no PJ's they fall asleep in their nice fancy clothes, hoping the day would continue in their dreams. The last words of their new friend Mabel repeating in their heads as they drift off.

"One day I'll have my own salon for you to visit. I'll make everyone feel as pretty as a rose."

Rose and Rodney wake up in their own beds with their own clothes on. They both look at the treasure chest confused. "Wow, was that a dream?" Rose whispers.

Rodney hops up out of bed. "Only one way to find out!"

Rodney kneels down next to the treasure chest and smiles at his sister. "Where should we go next?"

The End...

Thanks for going on that journey with us!

Learn More about Greenwood at PlayBlackWallStreet.com

Made in the USA
Middletown, DE
15 October 2023

40323997R00015